A Play

Junior Super Stars

Story by Carmel Reilly

People in the Play

Narrator

Nina

Eddie

Mrs Jacobs

Brad Hill

Lucy

Harry

Narrator

Eddie bounced the ball down the court.
He raced past one player, and then past another.

Nina

Go, Eddie!

Narrator

Within moments, Eddie was at the end of the court.
He threw the ball to Nina
and she passed it back to him.
He took aim at the basket. It was a difficult shot.
The ball slid around the top of the hoop
and fell through.

Nina

Great shot, Eddie! We've won!

Narrator

Eddie and Nina returned to their classroom.

Eddie

I love playing basketball.

I wish that I could play it all day.

Nina *(laughing)*

You are a great player, Eddie.

Eddie

You're good, too.

Nina

But I'm not nearly as good as you are.

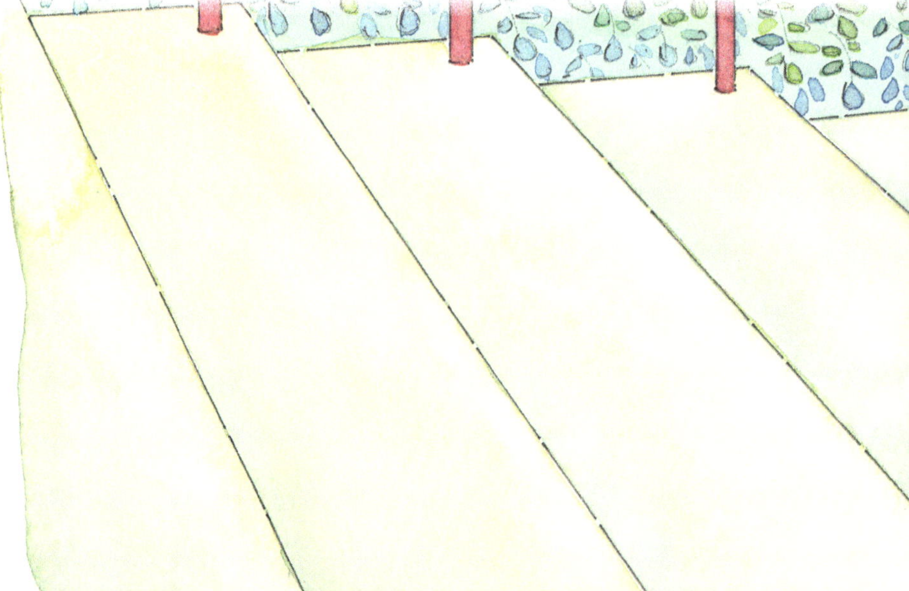

Narrator

Mrs Jacobs, the principal,
came into the classroom with a visitor.

Mrs Jacobs

Hello, everybody.
I'd like to introduce Brad Hill to you.
He is the captain
of the City Super Stars basketball team.

Eddie *(whispering to Nina)*

Brad Hill is fantastic! He's my favourite player.
I can't believe he's here!

Mrs Jacobs

Brad is starting a Junior Super Stars team.
He has come to look at our Grades 3 and 4 players.

Eddie *(whispering to Nina)*

Wow! I'd love to be in that team.

Brad Hill *(smiling)*

Thank you, Mrs Jacobs. Hello, boys and girls. I would like three players from your school to be in the team.

Mrs Jacobs

The teachers will choose our ten top players. Their names will be put on the gym noticeboard at lunchtime today.

Brad Hill

I'm going to work with this group tomorrow, so that I can select the three best players to be in the Junior Super Stars.

Narrator

The lunchtime bell rang,
and the children quickly put away their books.
Eddie and Nina raced across to the gym.

Nina

Eddie, look at all the children standing
at the noticeboard.

Eddie

I feel so nervous.

Lucy

Hooray! My name's on the list.

Harry

And so is mine!

Narrator

Eddie squeezed in between two taller boys
to look at the list.

Eddie

Nina! You're in Brad's group, too!
And so am I!

Narrator

The next morning, Eddie and Nina
and the other eight children arrived at school early.
Brad was already waiting for them in the gym.

Brad Hill

I'd like to begin with some basic throwing,
catching and defending.
First, I'll demonstrate some moves
with Eddie and Nina.

Narrator

Brad tried to pass the ball to Nina,
but Eddie leapt between them and grabbed it.

Brad Hill *(laughing)*

Nina, you'll need to keep your eye on Eddie.
He's very fast.

Narrator

Brad threw the ball to Nina again.
She moved quickly behind Eddie and snatched it.

Brad Hill *(nodding)*

That's much better, Nina.

Now the rest of you can work on those moves,

then we'll try something more difficult.

Narrator

Sometime later, Brad took a few of the children to the end of the court.

Brad Hill

Now, we're going to practise shooting baskets. Here, Eddie, you're first.

Narrator

Eddie took aim at the basket, but missed.

He tried again, but the ball spun around the edge of the hoop before it fell back towards him.

Eddie *(to himself)*

Oh, no!

Narrator

The children worked hard and fast for several minutes.

Brad Hill

I'd like this group to take a break now, while I work with the others.

Eddie *(to Nina, groaning)*

I was awful. I can't believe
that I'm playing so badly today.

Nina

Look at Harry. He's shot five baskets already.
And Lucy is really fast.

Eddie

Everyone is so good.
They're much better than me.
I don't think I'm going to get into this team.

Brad Hill

Thanks, everybody. Good work!
I'll meet you back here after school,
and tell you who is in the team.

Narrator

At home time, Nina, Eddie and the other children returned to the gym.

Eddie

I really want to be in the team, Nina,
but I played so badly this morning,
I'm sure I won't get in.

Nina

It's me who won't get in.
But I know you'll be all right.

Narrator

Brad and Mrs Jacobs arrived.

Brad Hill

First of all, I have to say
that you were all magnificent
and it was very hard to choose three players.
From Grade 4, I have chosen Harry and Lucy.

Lucy

It's our lucky day, Harry!

Harry *(grinning)*

You bet! Here – high five!

Brad Hill

And from Grade 3,

I have chosen Eddie.

Eddie *(jumping with excitement)*

Yes! I can't wait for the first game!

Nina *(patting Eddie on the back)*

Oh, Eddie! I knew you'd get into the team.
I'm going to come along and cheer for you!